The CATERPILLAR
and the POLLIWOG

Jack Kent

Prentice-Hall Books for Young Readers
A Division of Simon & Schuster, Inc., New York

To John Igo

Copyright © 1982 by Jack Kent
All rights reserved including the right of
reproduction in whole or in part in any form.
Published by Prentice-Hall Books for Young Readers
A Division of Simon & Schuster, Inc.
Simon & Schuster Building, Rockefeller Center
1230 Avenue of the Americas, New York, NY 10020

10 9 8 7 6 5 4

10 9 8 7 6 5   pbk

Prentice-Hall Books for Young Readers
is a trademark of Simon & Schuster, Inc.
Manufactured in the United States of America

Library of Congress Cataloging in Publication Data

Kent, Jack. The caterpillar and the polliwog.
SUMMARY: Impressed by the proud caterpillar's boast
that she will turn into a butterfly when she grows up,
a polliwog determines to watch the caterpillar very
carefully and turn into a butterfly too.
[1. Caterpillars—Fiction. 2. Tadpoles—Fiction] I. Title.
PZ7.K414Cat   [E]   82-7533
ISBN 0-13-120469-6   AACR2
ISBN 0-13-120478-5 pbk

Caterpillars aren't like other folks.
As ducks and hippopotamuses and you and I
get older, we get bigger. Especially
hippopotamuses.

But not caterpillars.

They turn into butterflies.

Turning into something else like that
is not a thing just anybody can do.

Down by the pond there lived a caterpillar
who was very proud of being different.
She bragged about it to her friends.
"When I grow up, I'm going to turn into
something else," she told the snail.

"That's nice," said the snail, who really
didn't care one way or the other.

"When I grow up, I'm going to turn into something else," she told the turtle.

"I don't blame you," said the turtle, who didn't much like wiggly things.

"When I grow up, I'm going to turn into something else," she told the polliwog.

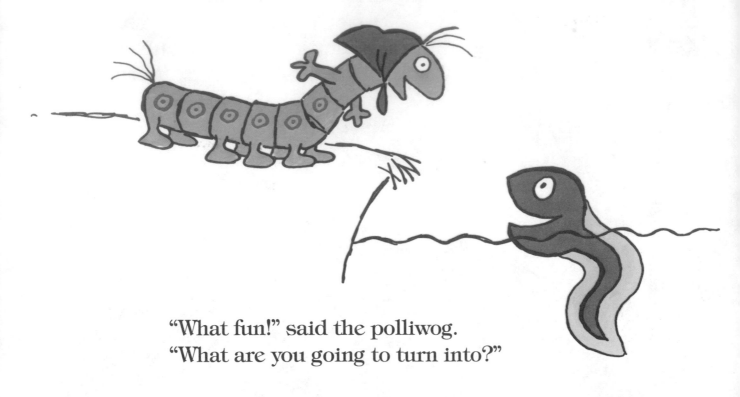

"What fun!" said the polliwog.
"What are you going to turn into?"

But the caterpillar hurried on her way, looking for someone else to tell her secret to.

"I wish *I* could turn into something else
when I grow up!" said the polliwog.

"You *will*," said the fish. "*All* polliwogs
do."

"What am I going to turn into?" the polliwog asked.

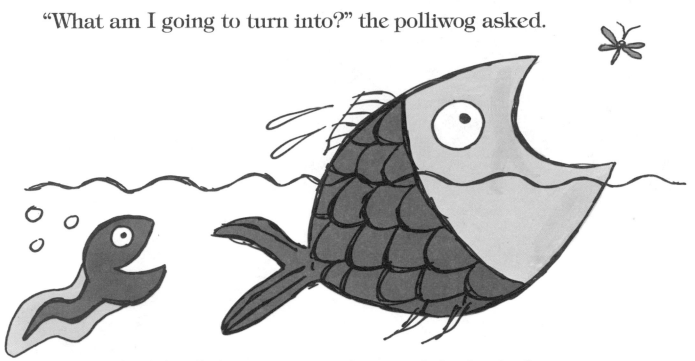

But the fish saw a tasty bug and dashed after it.

"When I grow up,"
said the caterpillar,
who had circled the pond
and was going around
for the second time,
"when I grow up," she
told the polliwog again,
"I'm going to turn
into something else."

"So am *I*!"
said the polliwog.

"*You?!*" The caterpillar was so surprised she almost fell into the pond.

"The fish said so," the polliwog told her. "Fish know things. They go to school."

The caterpillar was upset.
"I thought only caterpillars could do it,"
she said rather sadly.

"What are we going to turn into?" the
polliwog asked.

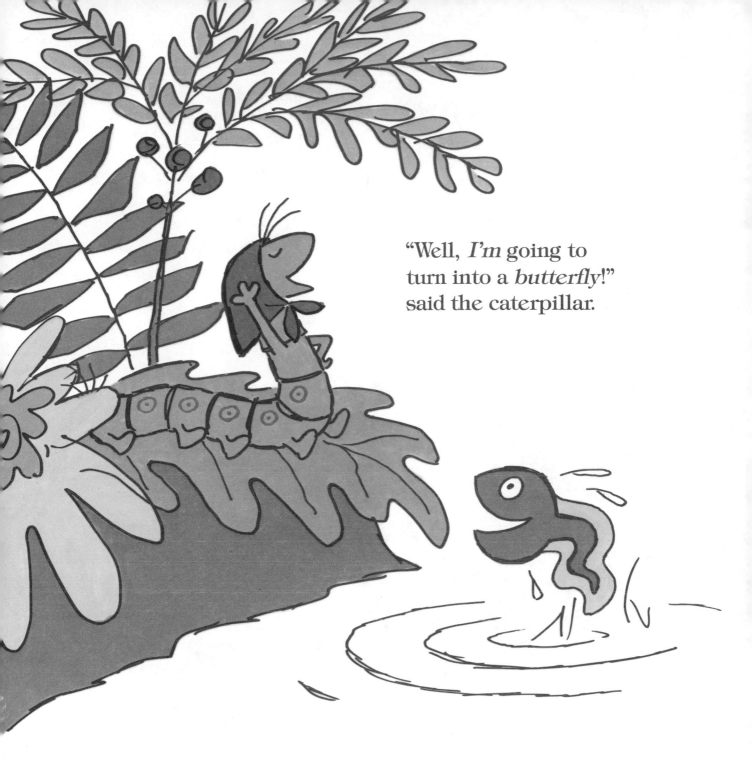

"Well, *I'm* going to
turn into a *butterfly!*"
said the caterpillar.

"Then I guess I will, too!" the polliwog
said happily. "What fun! Let's do it together!"

"All right," the caterpillar agreed, although she would rather have done it alone. "But I get to go first!"

The polliwog didn't mind. He wasn't at all sure how it was done. "I'll watch you," he said.

So when the time came,
the caterpillar started
to spin a cocoon.
"This is the tricky part,"
she said.

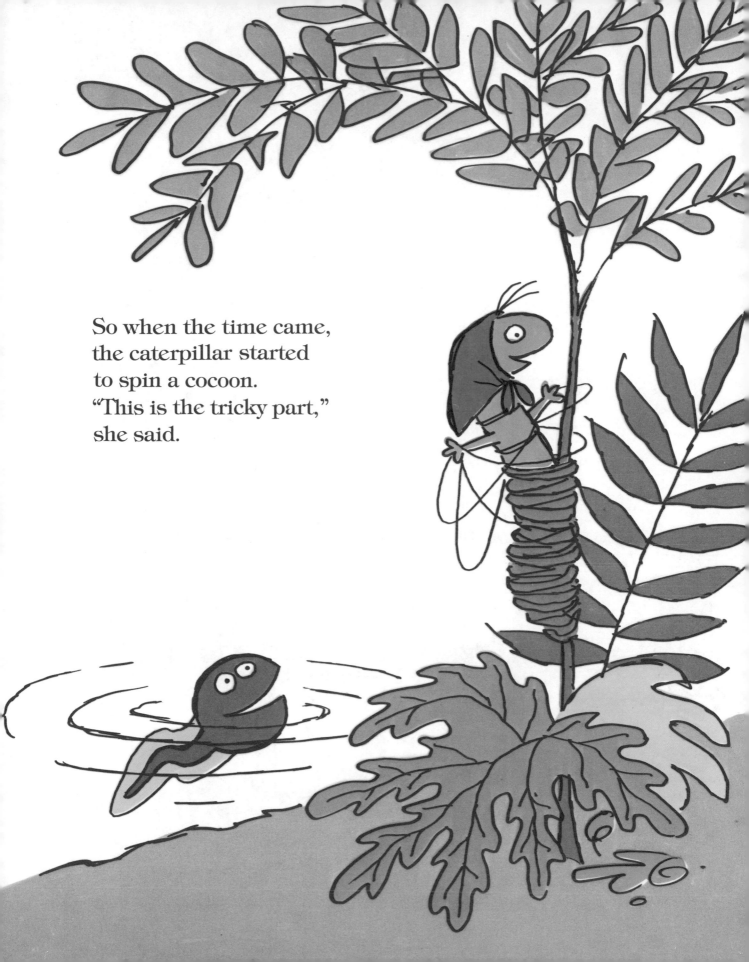

The polliwog watched
as the caterpillar spun.
Soon only her head
was uncovered.

"Now I have to close
the lid," she said.
"And when I come out,
I'll be a butterfly."

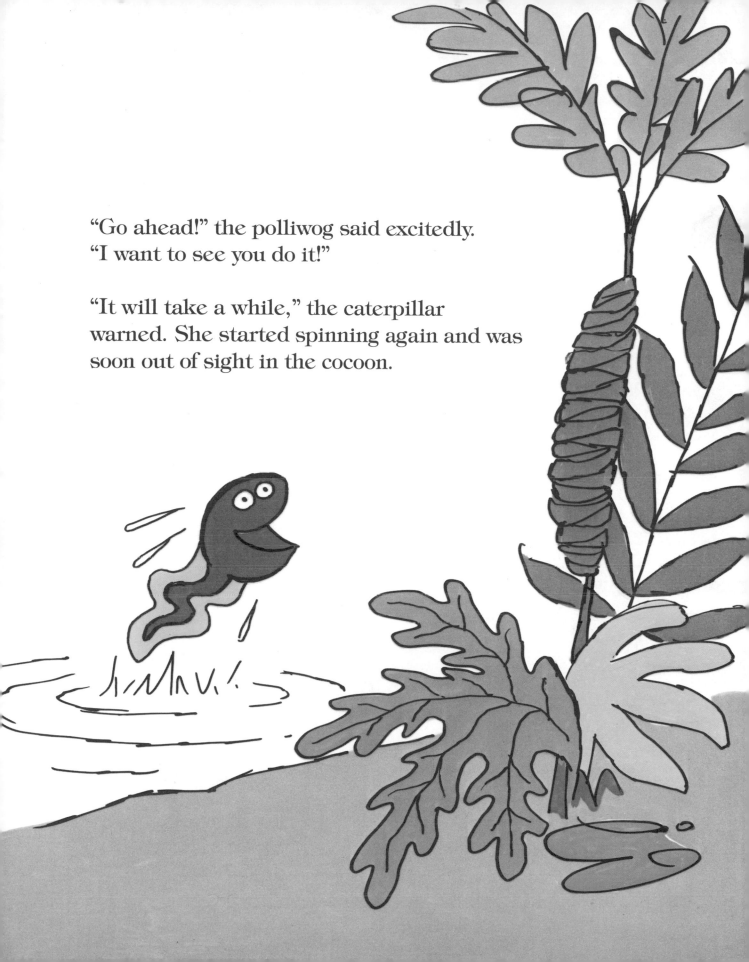

"Go ahead!" the polliwog said excitedly. "I want to see you do it!"

"It will take a while," the caterpillar warned. She started spinning again and was soon out of sight in the cocoon.

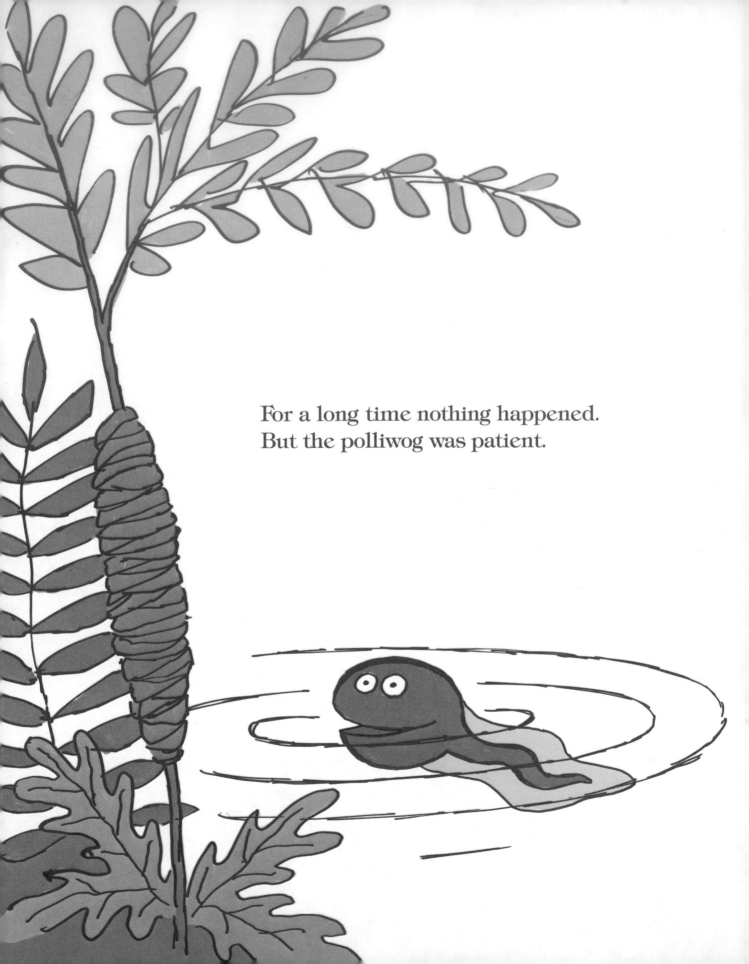

For a long time nothing happened.
But the polliwog was patient.

He watched
and watched
and watched,

for days
and days

and days.

At last there was activity in the cocoon. The end of it opened and, very slowly, the caterpillar climbed out.

Only she wasn't a caterpillar anymore.
She was a *butterfly*! A beautiful yellow
butterfly!

The polliwog was so excited he hopped up and down with delight!

He *hopped*! Up and down! Like a *frog*!

"I was so busy watching *you*," he said, "I didn't notice what was happening to *me*!"

"You're a very handsome frog," the butterfly
said, as she flew off to try her new wings.

But the frog was puzzled. "I thought I was going to be a butterfly," he said.

A caterpillar wiggled by.
"When I grow up,"
he said proudly to the frog,
"I'm going to turn into
something else!"

But the frog wasn't listening.

He was admiring his
reflection in the water.
"I *am*, you know,
a *very* handsome frog!" he said.